Dear Parent:
Your child's love of reading starts here!

Every child learns to read in a different way and at his or her own speed. Some go back and forth between reading levels and read favorite books again and again. Others read through each level in order. You can help your young reader improve and become more confident by encouraging his or her own interests and abilities. From books your child reads with you to the first books he or she reads alone, there are I Can Read Books for every stage of reading:

SHARED READING
Basic language, word repetition, and whimsical illustrations, ideal for sharing with your emergent reader

BEGINNING READING
Short sentences, familiar words, and simple concepts for children eager to read on their own

READING WITH HELP
Engaging stories, longer sentences, and language play for developing readers

READING ALONE
Complex plots, challenging vocabulary, and high-interest topics for the independent reader

ADVANCED READING
Short paragraphs, chapters, and exciting themes for the perfect bridge to chapter books

I Can Read Books have introduced children to the joy of reading since 1957. Featuring award-winning authors and illustrators and a fabulous cast of beloved characters, I Can Read Books set the standard for beginning readers.

A lifetime of discovery begins with the magical words "I Can Read!"

Visit www.icanread.com for information on enriching your child's reading experience.

Charlotte's Web™

WILBUR'S PRIZE

Adapted by Jennifer Frantz

Illustrated by Aleksey and Olga Ivanov

Based on the Motion Picture

Screenplay by Susanna Grant and Karey Kirkpatrick

Based on the book by E. B. White

HarperCollins*Publishers*

Charlotte's Web: Wilbur's Prize

™ & © 2006 Paramount Pictures Corp. All rights reserved. Printed in the United States of America. No part of this book may be used or reproduced in any manner whatsoever without written permission except in the case of brief quotations embodied in critical articles and reviews. For information address HarperCollins Children's Books, a division of HarperCollins Publishers, 1350 Avenue of the Americas, New York, NY 10019. www.icanread.com

Library of Congress catalog card number: 2006920331
ISBN-10: 0-06-088284-0 (trade bdg.) — ISBN-13: 978-0-06-088284-6 (trade bdg.)
ISBN-10: 0-06-088283-2 (pbk.) — ISBN-13: 978-0-06-088283-9 (pbk.)

First Edition

It was the first day of the County Fair!
Everyone at Zuckerman's farm
was busy getting ready.

Ties were tied.

Pies were packed.

Jams were jarred.

And Wilbur the pig
was bathed in buttermilk.

He *would* need to look his best
if he was going to win
the blue ribbon at the fair.

Wilbur's friends in the barn
knew winning the blue ribbon
was important.

It was Wilbur's chance
to show how special he was.
Then the Zuckermans would
keep him on the farm forever!

Charlotte was planning to weave
a very special web at the fair.
She had to find the perfect word
to describe Wilbur.

Charlotte convinced Templeton

to come along and help.

Finding trash was his specialty.

And old wrappers and boxes

were full of words.

The friends arrived at the fair.

It was unlike any place

they had ever been!

Colorful tents crowded the grounds.

Sweet smells drifted through the air.

And a giant wheel spun in the sky!

15

Wilbur settled into his pen.

In the stall next door

was the biggest pig

Charlotte had ever seen!

16

His name was Uncle.

Charlotte knew that Uncle

would be hard to beat.

Wilbur was nervous.

But Charlotte calmed his fears.

"The *finest* pig is not always
the *fattest* pig," she said.

Then Charlotte told Templeton

to go out and find a good word—

FAST!

The fairground was littered
with trash and bits of food.
It was Templeton's dream come true!

But he had a job to do.

Templeton spotted a newspaper.

But others spotted Templeton, too. . . .

Two feisty crows were watching.

And they loved to chase Templeton!

Templeton had to think fast.

"Yoo hoo!" Templeton called.

The crows dove after Templeton,

but were quickly tangled up.

Templeton scurried to the pigpen,
and gave Charlotte a scrap of paper
that was full of words.

24

Charlotte looked at the paper
and grew quiet.
Then her eyes lit up.
She had found the perfect word!

Charlotte worked on the web for hours.
When she finished, Wilbur looked up
and saw the word . . . "HUMBLE."

"But I don't think I deserve it,"
Wilbur said.

Charlotte smiled at her friend.

"Then it *is* perfect," she said.

The next morning the judges
would decide which pig
was the best in the fair.

But Wilbur no longer cared
if he won the blue ribbon.

Wilbur already had

the best prize of all . . .

the very best friends

any pig could imagine.

And no word could ever describe just how lucky Wilbur felt.